GRANTED

A tale of Captain Percy Coyle
and Codename: Blue

by Gregory Adams

UNBIDDEN THOUGHTS

Unbidden Thoughts Press

Norwood, Massachusetts

2025

Granted

A tale of Captain Percy Coyle and Codename: Blue

ISBN: 979-8-9928917-3-7

Published by Unbidden Thoughts Press

Norwood, Massachusetts

Printed in the United States of America

For All My Readers, Ever, Anywhere

Thank you

I

The telephone gave an angry, restless buzz.

Percy Coyle was awake at once.

The phone stood on a small cradle on a nightstand beside his bed, and it only went off once every few years. It was a direct line to the President of the United States.

"Percy, sorry to wake you," the President said. "But the boys in SAC are telling me we have something that wasn't there before. Sounds like it might be in your province."

The President was mixed race, and that both delighted and amazed Percy. Such a thing had been entirely unthinkable when he had entered the service.

"Thank you, sir," he said. He sat up in bed and swung his feet down to the carpeted floor. He didn't have to worry about disturbing a spouse; Percy lived alone.

"I'll be right in. And as I mentioned when we were introduced, sir, there's no need for you to call me yourself. I'm just another soldier."

Percy could hear the President smile. "It's tradition, Percy, and my pleasure. Give my best to Big Blue."

"Will do, sir," Percy said as he disconnected.

It was a newer tradition, to be sure. Hayes never came and knocked on Percy's door, and he'd helped that President twice.

Percy could already sense that Big Blue was in the room with him, likely seated in the high-backed chair in the southeast corner of the large bedroom that was his favorite. Percy knew it even before he saw the faint glow of the being's large yellow eyes.

II

"It's a satellite," the DIA man explained. "Or maybe a space station. It's quite sizable."

Percy was in the back of a long limousine, part of a motorcade speeding to Langley. The spinning lights of their police escort gave a surreal impression to the scene, but Percy supposed that was him showing his age. The Defense Intelligence Agency man was clearly intimidated by Code Name: Blue, who reclined beside Percy, taking no part in the debriefing, because the djinn knew all this already.

"The UFO appeared just three hours ago, in a geosynchronous orbit over the

Southeastern United States. Florida would be the most exact positioning we could give at this time."

"Any communication from it yet?" Percy asked.

The DIA man smirked. "Communication hasn't stopped, actually. One individual—American by his speech—we guess about thirty years old. He refuses to use a video channel of any kind, although we have to assume he has the means. Here's a transcript of what's been broadcast to us."

Percy shook his head. "Are other people seeing this?" he asked. "On their televisions? Their computers? Or their telephones—their smart telephones?"

"No, sir," the DIA man replied. "His beef—well, he has many—but his main beef seems to be with the United States Government. He called the FBI offices in Miami and was transferred to us when we put the UFO and what he was saying

8

together. He's been saying all this into their phone lines."

"Boy, he does go on," Percy remarked, fanning the pages he'd been handed.

"He is claiming that if we do not comply with his demands, he'll begin tungsten rod bombardment of the Eastern Seaboard." He looked up sheepishly. "Are you familiar with this sort of weapon?"

"It's got 'bombardment' in the name—I assume it's a kind of missile or nuclear bomb or some such? Launched from space?" Percy could see from the man's expression that this description was wrong, and the man was aching to explain, but there wasn't time.

"I get it; he has a powerful weapon, and he'll kill a lot of people if he fires it."

The DIA man nodded.

"Okay, what else have we been doing so far?"

"Mostly we've been stalling him, but frankly, I'm not sure why he hasn't done what he's threatened, because we've given him nothing concrete yet." As he spoke, the limo jumped as it passed over the tracks of the sliding gate into Langley Field. "We suspect he may not have the weapons he claims."

Percy shook his head. "No, he has the weapon. They always have the weapon. But he certainly missed something." Percy was quiet for a heartbeat, then said, "He can't get down."

Blue smiled from beneath his oversized wraparound sunglasses. "HE CANNOT GET DOWN!" he echoed in his vast, rumbling voice. Then he laughed so ferociously that the limousine shook.

Percy was long accustomed to such outbursts, but his heart went out to the DIA man as he turned sheet white.

Blue could vanish anytime he wanted, and Percy sometimes went years without seeing the djinn. Blue was sticking around now, and that wasn't a surprise. The djinn's presence reassured the President and his staff, and that reassurance could be seen as part of the conditions of Percy's long-ago and swiftly formulated wish.

Percy had been afforded a long time to consider his situation. Djinn could clearly do the impossible; Percy's own long life was more than evidence of this.

And he'd seen things—things the wishes of others had conjured—things that boggled the mind, even more so as each new discovery of this dazzling modern age pulled back the curtain a bit further on how the universe operated.

"Okay, just get me on the telephone with this one," Percy said, relieved that this trouble could be solved remotely. He hated flying. "No need to fly anywhere. I'll talk him down."

"We can do that on the plane," the DIA man said. He began to say, "The President wants you nearby," but was drowned out as Big Blue said the same words along with him, only far, far more loudly and with tremendous mirth.

III

When President Kennedy had been in office, he'd arranged for Percy to meet with several scientists, theologians, and other scholars, hoping to get a bead on whatever Blue actually was. The young President had great faith in the American science of the age—a well-founded faith, Percy supposed, given the success of the space program.

Percy had forgotten most of these talks, they being simply lengthier conversations about matters Percy had few facts about. There was one interview, with scientist-turned-novelist Carl Sagan, that stayed with Percy—perhaps even haunted him.

The meeting, held in an informal setting in one of the many federal properties in Virginia, involved comfortable chairs and pots of steaming hot tea. There were wafers and other snacks on a porcelain dish on a fine doily and that on a dark-stained colonial end table, but Professor Sagan's inquiries came too swiftly to allow Percy time to chew.

Sagan, a turtlenecked, inquisitive presence that smelt of tobacco and positively glowed with energy, had begun by asking many of the usual questions people asked when they first met Percy—but Sagan asked these without the smirking disbelief Percy had endured for a century. The scientist accepted right away that Percy was telling the truth, perhaps because the President (who did not join them for this talk, and to Percy's knowledge never met Sagan) so clearly believed it.

"I wonder about your brain," Professor Sagan said. Percy was taken aback: the conversation had moved on from the subject of Big Blue and onto questions about Percy's experiences and memories of over one hundred years of life. Percy always answered these as best he was able, but there was little he knew that he would consider fascinating. The last century was well documented, after all. And in fairness, he couldn't recall his distant youth with much clarity. That had seemed natural to him, but Sagan was putting this in a new perspective.

"The human brain has evolved to hold a certain amount of memory," he said. "Just as the human body lives for a certain amount of time. It's clear that the djinni has altered your physiology, perhaps a massive degree, to preserve you so well across such a long period, and I wonder if that extends to the actual physical makeup of your brain?" The professor was staring at Percy's forehead with unnerving intensity. "The Russians are developing a Hahn Echo machine, and I wonder what such imaging would show us about your limbic system. Not to put it too bluntly, I wonder how you're able to hold a gallon of memories in a pint glass of grey matter."

Sagan smiled at this, but Percy felt himself turning a little green.

He'd often speculated about what might have been going on inside of him to compensate for his being a centenarian with the appearance and characteristics of a twenty-six-year-old, but that didn't make the topic of 'massive' alterations to his body any more comfortable to discuss.

IV

"Good morning, sir," Percy said into the microphone. He was on a plane headed to an undisclosed location where the President and his family had been taken, presumably far away from the East Coast. This had become routine: a credible Code Name: Blue threat emerged, and Percy found himself shuttled to close proximity to the President as a safety measure.

It was believed that Percy couldn't be killed, and, therefore, any location he was at became that much safer, although Percy himself thought this an absurd interpretation of the circumstances.

"My name is Percy Coyle, and I am a captain in the United States Army."

"You're not the President!" the enraged man in orbit high above Florida replied. His southern accent was pronounced, and his fury caused the speaker to crackle.

Percy was undaunted. "That's true, sir, but we believe that this development falls under my expertise. Just a few questions, and if I'm wrong, well, I'm sure whoever follows after me will be more agreeable to your expectations." The angry man in the satellite started to interrupt but choked on his words when Percy said, "So, was the djinn you found in a lamp or a bottle?"

The transcript would show seventeen seconds of silence before the man answered, hesitantly, "It was a genie. It was in a bottle."

"That's interesting. We haven't seen a bottle in almost fifty years. Mine was in a bottle also. Was yours blue?"

"No, he wasn't blue," came the reply. "Red. Red like fire."

The DIA man flipped through a binder filled with laminated images and illustrations—there were no photographs of djinn—but Percy waved him off. He knew what red meant, as well as anyone alive did.

"Okay, that's one angry djinn you have there. You might call it a genie, and that's fine, but they prefer djinn, and manners are important to these beings. Now, is the red djinn still with you?"

"No, he left. What was your name again?"

"I'm Captain Percy Coyle. I work for the federal government."

"How come I never heard of you?"

"What I do is top secret," Percy said. "All of this sort of thing, this magic business, is top secret. I do have to ask, are you a Christian?"

"Yes, sir, I am."

"Okay, that's fine. Djinn were created by God from smokeless fire, whereas He created us from mud and earth. You've committed no great sin in dealing with such a being, but I do recommend bringing it up at your next confession. I'm not one to judge, but it seems like you may have acted a bit selfishly."

"I don't go to church much anymore," the voice replied.

All of this was very encouraging for Percy, but it was far too early to feel confident. The demands had stopped, and he hadn't once mentioned firing a tungsten rod barrage. Percy felt he'd talked the man down enough to move on to more personal questions.

"Maybe I can know your name now, sir? We are part of a very exclusive club, after all."

"I'm Timothy Dauterive. I'm from Sarasota County."

"Thank you, Timothy. I've been to Florida—it's great country, especially on the Gulf side."

Beside Percy, the DIA man punched Timothy's name into a computer, and the man's life history began spewing out of the printer.

"Thank you," Timothy said, clearly perplexed by the direction the conversation was taking.

"So why a satellite?" Percy asked.

Seven seconds of silence. "It was the genie's idea, I guess," Timothy confessed. "I just wanted to change things, make America better, and he said I was going about it wrong."

"He said if you wish for one thing to be the way you want it, then wish is gone. But if you wish for a way to make things the way you want them, you can change whatever you want to change. Does that sound about right?"

"Yeah, he said something like that. This space station here—I can, I don't know, hold the whole world hostage. He said no one else had anything like it. I'd be the man in charge."

"Yup, I see how that makes sense. Did that take all three wishes? The space station?"

Eleven seconds of silence. "It did. One to make it, one to put the weapons on it…"

"And one to get up there," Percy said. "It's not your fault, Thomas. The red ones—they are angry, and that anger makes them—well, duplicitous isn't too strong a word." He snuck a glance at Blue, who might take exception at unflattering, even if true, comments about his kind. Blue didn't return the glance, seemingly absorbed in the dials and switches of the onboard radar station of the C-130, much to the consternation of a naval officer standing nearby. But no one asked the hulking djinni to stop touching things.

"Now, you say you're a Christian, so I need you to understand this: djinn are not devils or demons, so you haven't committed a mortal sin in dealing with one of these fellows. But please understand that, like devils, these red djinns have a powerful dislike for mortals. Well, to be honest, it is the dislike that makes them red, but you couldn't know that; this isn't a thing they teach in school or church."

Percy was starting to enjoy this. He'd favored a Southern accent in his youth but had learned to disguise it when he'd enrolled in the Army of the Potomac and had continued to do so ever since, even when he'd met Southern Presidents, like Carter or the second Johnson, the one from Texas. This Timothy character was so unabashedly Southern that Percy felt the old words and patterns returning as they spoke.

"Was yours red?" Timothy asked.

"No, Timothy, I was fortunate. I got a blue one. We didn't always see eye to eye, but he didn't mistreat me in any way." As far as I know, Percy thought, but did not confess. "I'm of a mind, Timothy, that believes you want to get down from there. Back to Earth."

Timothy began to rage again, but only at about twenty percent of his peak fury. "I'm not giving this place up until they do what I ask."

"I understand how you feel," Percy said. "But you do want to get back here, back to solid ground." Percy paused. "Do you have gravity in that place?"

"No," Timothy replied, putting great frustration into the syllable. "My boots stick to the floor, with Velcro, it's called? You know the stuff? Sounds like I'm tearing my pants every step. Mostly I float around. It's not bad," he added without much conviction.

"Okay, now how about food? Water?" Percy paused, silently exploring how to best serve delicacy with his next question, then went with, "Facilities?"

"Yes! Of course this thing has a toilet!" Timothy replied.

Big Blue laughed.

"Who the hell is that?" Timothy shouted, rage suddenly nearing eighty percent of peak.

Percy sighed. "That's Blue. I don't know his actual name; these beings are careful about their names. He's why I asked if the red was still with you. Blue is the djinn I found. He stuck around, and he helps me sometimes."

This wasn't entirely true.

In their long association, Blue had provided exactly one service: convincing every important federal personage, beginning with President Lincoln's Secretary of War, that Percy Coyle's claim to the supernatural was gospel truth, and Blue accomplished that simply by being present.

An almost ten-foot-tall, blue-skinned, yellow-eyed, black-bearded being with a lower body that often trailed away into a swirling funnel of blue smoke was a difficult sight to dismiss.

"Blue is my partner in our work," Percy continued. "I was born in 1844, in Virginia, as I've said. When the South rose up, I left my home and went north, to fight for the Union. This may put you and me at odds, I suppose, but I never shot anyone, so I certainly didn't serve with any distinction.

"I was under General Tucker when I found the bottle. We were tearing up railroad tracks in Maryland, and there it was, buried in the ground under the rails. A blue bottle with silver—filigree, I guess—all over it. It looked expensive, and when I picked it up, it felt like it was made of clay instead of glass, and there was something inside of it. It was heavy."

"Mine too!" Timothy replied. "It was in this house. The lady who owned it had died, and we were going to demo the place and…"

Percy leaned back in his own seat and waited for Timothy to run out of story. Eventually, his turn to talk would come.

GREGORY ADAMS

GRANTED

A TALE OF
PERCY COYLE
AND
CODENAME:
BLUE

V

Carl Sagan hadn't met Blue. There was no emergency, and Blue kept his noncrucial appearances to a minimum. As with many conversations, Blue's absence had filled the room beyond even what his own overlarge form would have accomplished.

"Where does this djinni"—nailing the pronunciation, something Percy hadn't done to Blue's satisfaction until two decades into their association—"go when he's not here? Not back into the bottle, surely?" Sagan asked.

Percy had no idea where the djinni went or what it did when it wasn't attending to him, and in their years of association, that speculation had grown to include having no idea where else the djinn might be even when it was attending to him. The idea that Blue must abide by any known laws of physics was one Percy had given up on long ago.

But Sagan made it clear that he positively believed Blue to be understandable. "We just don't know yet how he does what he does," Sagan said. "In the infancy of our race, we didn't know how the sun burned, or how the stars moved, or how we remember what happened yesterday. It was all magic to us for most of our existence as a species. Now we understand a little of the truth of these processes, but not all there is to know. The djinn simply understands the workings of creation better than we do."

"But he grants wishes," Percy had said. "He has a will of his own, but he does what I ask him to."

"Then make him appear," Sagan had said.

"I can't," Percy replied. "Not without wrongly discharging my duty to the Union."

"So, he does what he wants to do," Sagan answered. "Or, if we accept that his presence gives proof to the presence of a Creator, then he does what the Creator wishes. But whatever it is that determines the djinni's behavior is just another discoverable unknown. At this point, we simply don't understand why Blue does what he does any more than we understand the how of his actions. But I have absolute faith that all of this can be explained and will one day be understood. Perhaps if the American Union persists long enough, you'll get to know the answer."

Sagan had been buoyant, but a shadow fell over his expression when he added: "I envy you, and your long life. But then again, it may be a foolish envy."

They'd spent the remaining hour pleasantly enough, and Percy had never seen

Professor Carl Sagan again. He also never saw the professor's report and couldn't say what conclusions had been reached, if any.

VI

"That's a hell of a story, Timothy," Percy said almost twenty minutes later. "Hell of a story. Mine's not that different, all in all. Had me a bit more luck in finding a blue instead of a red, but there's nothing for that. Not like these bottles are labeled."

"Now, I know I've been riding on my Virginia accent, but it's time for some truth, here. I was Virginia born, in what's still Virginia. And I was a Union boy. I was just a corporal in the Army of the Potomac, and I'm sad to say the only action I saw was dropping my rifle and tearing like hell out of First Manassas.

"To my good fortune I wasn't shot for cowardice, and mostly I got marched around in circles for the next few months before I found the bottle in the rail bed as I'd described. When I saw it was a genie"—Blue gave a stifled cough, less interruptive than the thunder of a close lightning strike—Percy corrected himself. "I saw it was a djinn like in Arabian Nights, and well, I made my wish. My one wish."

"To live forever?" Timothy asked. "Is that how you're so old and all?"

"No, sir," Percy answered. "My shameful behavior at my only engagement weighed on me, and you know, I was there because the thing mattered to me. The splitting of the Union, and the plight of the slaves. It all mattered to me, and I wanted to preserve one and fix the other. But I wanted to do it. I didn't want this magic blue angel to do it with a nod of his head."

And maybe I didn't trust him was left unsaid for the ten-thousandth time in the telling of this tale.

"So I made my wish. I said I wanted a long life in service to the Union. And he said granted."

"So, what happened?" Timothy asked. "Did Lee surrender next day or something?"

"Oh God, no," Percy said. "This was early on—before Vicksburg, before Gettysburg, even before Wilderness. McClellan was still in command, and my tired feet from marching in circles told me that man wasn't going to win any wars.

"No, I didn't feel any different and the war didn't end, but Blue didn't vanish either. He went with me to my commander, and then we went to General Tucker, and then I was shipped by train to McClellan. There it almost ended, because he put a terrible pressure on me to end the war and—get this—wish him

President, and not in that order, let me tell you.

"Anyway, President Lincoln got wind of the matter, and I was brought to him over McClellan's objections, and that's where my life took shape."

"I'm not sure I'm believing any of this," Timothy said.

"Timothy, hear me out," Percy insisted.

He'd read what the DIA man had found on Timothy Dauterive, and thought it was time to put that knowledge into play.

"You're a high school dropout who worked off the books for a Polk County demolition company, and now you're on an orbital weapons platform with your finger on the trigger of a gun that could erase everything south of Lake Okeechobee with one shot—so please, just take me at my word for a minute or two, alright?"

Percy took the responding silence as permission to continue. "President Lincoln didn't ask for the things General McClellan did. He never asked for anything from Blue or me, and I knew the man through the war and for the remainder of his days. He said if things like Blue were out there, and if they could be compelled by any mortal who discovered them, well then there was only one force on Earth that could counter the happenstance of their will."

"God?" Timothy asked.

"President Lincoln used words carefully, and I was quoting his exact words. He said, 'on Earth,' not 'of Heaven.' Say what you will about the man, but he was terribly wise. He forewent the swift solution and said to me, 'Captain Percival Coyle, you serve the Union, and as your Supreme Commander, I put you in the following service: you are to use those two remaining wishes only in defense and preservation of the Union, and only against otherworldly forces.' Do you see it, Timothy? My job is to use my wishes to prevent or repair damages done by folk such as you. I have kept my word through all of this time, against every terrible moment that was made by the will of men, and men alone.

"I left Abraham Lincoln shot, I didn't undo Pearl Harbor, I let John Kennedy die in Dallas. I let Vietnam run on and on, and I didn't stop those planes in '01 because Abraham Lincoln had told me I could only use my wishes to stop people like you."

"So wait," Timothy said, wrestling with the message. "You have two wishes left?"

"I do," Percy said. "Fire those rods and I will ask Blue here to send them back to you. You'll die alone in space, and not one person in Florida or anywhere else you wish to target will even know you were up there."

"Okay, wish me down then," Timmy said with great urgency. He'd clearly lost his battle with fear of being stranded.

"I will not do that," Percy said, his voice iron. "I will not use my wishes to save you."

This was always the worst part—the most terrible part: when the people who had put themselves in horrible straits through greed, selfishness, and hate begged Percy to save them.

Abraham Lincoln had never begged.

Edith Wilson had asked, and only once: Will you help my husband? Percy had wept at her choice of words—will you, not can you, because of course, he could have. But Percy refused.

Franklin Roosevelt had never asked to walk.

Hell, god-damn Richard Nixon had never asked Percy to wish his troubles away. Every President since Lincoln had met

Blue and understood that the djinn could fix their problems, but they hadn't risen to the office of President of the United States so some second-rate angel could fix the problems people had made. They saw Percy and Blue for what they were: tools to clear up trouble that wasn't of human design, and nothing more.

VII

"I'm sitting with a man from the Defense Intelligence Agency," Percy said. "These people are like the CIA and Homeland Security on steroids, and they are turning every resource, EVERY RESOURCE, to getting you down safely."

The DIA man, on the phone and muttering in what sounded like Mandarin, nodded and gave a thumbs up.

"They'll get you down. You and I will meet in person. I am looking forward to that."

This was Percy's first intentional lie, and it was only half a falsehood.

Timothy might sound like a genuine moron but there was no other living soul who had entered into a contract as he had, and such rare fraternity was something he genuinely missed. However the conversation, mandated by Presidential order, would be unpleasant.

"Okay these CIA guys on steroids have twelve hours," Timothy said, as if confirming Percy's unspoken dislike of their imminent meeting.

"Timothy, listen to me," Percy said. "You can not make demands on us. You are out of wishes."

"I still have this gun!" Timothy insisted.

"Yes, but you're out of choices," Percy said. "You have no wishes remaining while I have two. The red is laughing at you as he waits for you to die of thirst, hunger or asphyxiation. It's Tuesday morning, and there's only one way this ends with you seeing Sunday: You cooperate with these men, and they get you down. Then they take care of you. Likely for the rest of your life."

"How's that?" Timothy asked. "They'll put me in jail?"

"Not jail, Timothy, but they do keep us close. There are few people alive who have had congress with these beings. They'll want to know every detail; you won't believe the detail they'll get into. They'll run a thousand tests on you. They'll want to know, Why you, and How has it changed you? And they'll need your cooperation to get it all accurate.

"I've seen it before Timothy, several times. We get over this matter with you threatening to destroy everyone you don't like, and you'll see some benefit come out of it, I promise you. You'll not have to swing a crowbar for a payday again or come home covered in plaster dust." You'll never see home again, most likely Percy thought, but again he left these unpleasant thoughts unspoken.

Beside him, Blue sat idle, clearly bored. A red light began to flash; they were descending. Percy stayed on the phone with Timothy until it was time to disembark. He was kept busy with carrot and stick, but by the time he passed the handling of Timothy over to someone who could address the technical issues the man's rescue, Percy felt like he had matters in hand.

IIX

"Do you know him, this red?" Percy asked Big Blue as they crossed to the elevator that would take them down to whatever room had been prepared for them near the President's own quarters. There they would wait until Timothy Dauterive was safely off his orbital weapons platform.

It was likely a futile question. Blue hardly ever spoke. To Percy's complete lack of surprise, the hulking djinn gave a wry smile and a shrug.

Are you the red? Percy asked inwardly. *Is all of this your doing?*

The conversation with Professor Sagan had shaken Percy up. Since then, he had begun to look at his relationship with Blue differently.

Every other human being he'd encountered who'd had a wish granted had suffered in some way; many had died as a result. He'd been waiting for the shoe to drop with his own situation, but it never had.

In a century and a half, Percy had never encountered a conundrum that required the use of one of his two remaining wishes.

To my knowledge—that was the unspoken, paranoid refrain.

Some speculated that if a second wish were used to undo the first, perhaps that meant the second wish had never truly been discharged—its necessity having been erased. Percy had heard the argument more times than he could count but had never fully grasped it.

After all, unless he had explicitly wished to travel back in time—and to his knowledge, he hadn't—wouldn't he remember making such a wish?

And barring such a specific command, why would Blue resolve his wishes in a way that erased their execution?

Most unsettling of all: why would Blue, of all beings, want his servitude to Percy to stretch on indefinitely?

Percy couldn't discount paranoia, a condition he'd been diagnosed with by more than one military doctor over the years. He'd outlived them all and watched their certainty driven under by progress they could never have imagined.

If he was paranoid, or suffering from some other form of mental illness, it manifested in ways he found to be strangely specific.

Many nights, or in periods of long isolation, Percy was haunted by half-remembered crises—too many crises to account for the two wishes he routinely traded on. These flashes of déjà vu, unmoored from anything Percy understood as history and perhaps the products of his overstuffed, overclocked brain, were vivid, persistent, and maddeningly incomplete: steel monsters cresting San Juan Hill; U.S. currency bearing the faces of Poe, Whitman, and Steinbeck; a modern New York where no building rose above three stories; a combative meeting with President Rothschild…

The elevator doors opened. They were far underground. Blue had disappeared, something Percy had failed to notice while lost in his brown study. A Secret Serviceman with a machine gun dangling from a strap waited to escort Percy to his quarters.

Do I actually have any wishes left? Percy asked himself as they walked down the narrow corridor, patriotic emblems lining the white walls. If not, what is Blue doing to me?

"So he does what he wants to do," Sagan had said. "But we simply don't understand what that is any more than we do the how."

Percy's attendant opened the door to his quarters, which Percy knew would be remarkably similar to his own home in Virginia. Someone in the DIA thought it would relax Percy if his many safe locations looked like his residence.

In the instant before the light was switched on, Percy thought he saw yellow eyes glowing from the high-backed padded chair in the corner, but once the lights were on, he could see that the chair was plainly empty.

ABOUT THE AUTHOR

Gregory Adams writes strange stories and unbidden thoughts. His work explores the surreal edge of the everyday, blending dark humor, quiet horror, and literary sharpness. Influenced by  George Orwell, Shirley Jackson, and Richard Aikman, Adams crafts fiction that confronts the world as it is—and hints at what might be just beneath.

He is the author of One Day in Hell, The River Above, and Season of the W.I.T.C.H. all available on Amazon.com. He lives in Massachusetts, where he divides his time between writing, dog walking, and quietly resisting the expected.

Gregory's latest fiction can be found at GregoryAdamsFiction.com, gregoryadams.substack.com, and on Medium under Gregory Adams Fiction.

More fiction from Gregory Adams

Had Roald Dahl and H.P. Lovecraft managed to combine
across time and space, the result would have been a creature
of unspeakable hideousness and malevolence. Fortunately,
we can skip the hideousness and malevolence and enjoy the
stories of Gregory Adams, whose work provides the sharp
jolt of dark humor that marks the best of Dahl's work
wrapped around the existential terror at the heart of
Lovecraft's. You'll scream—with delight!
—Seamus Cooper
author of *The Mall of Cthulhu* and *Terror at The Shore*

Available in paperback and Kindle editions
on Amazon.com